D1112781

Fairy Chase

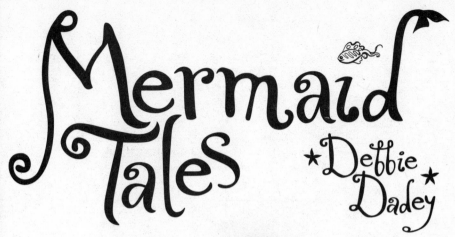

Mermaid Tales

Debbie Dadey

Illustrated by
Tatevik Avakyan

BOOK 18

Fairy Chase

ALADDIN

NEW YORK   LONDON   TORONTO   SYDNEY   NEW DELHI

ALADDIN

An imprint of Simon & Schuster Children's Publishing Division

1230 Avenue of the Americas, New York, New York 10020

This Aladdin hardcover edition May 2018

Text copyright © 2018 by Debbie Dadey

Illustrations copyright © 2018 by Tatevik Avakyan

Also available in an Aladdin paperback edition.

For information about special discounts for bulk purchases, please contact Simon & Schuster Special Sales at 1-866-506-1949 or business@simonandschuster.com.

The Simon & Schuster Speakers Bureau can bring authors to your live event. For more information or to book an event contact the Simon & Schuster Speakers Bureau at 1-866-248-3049 or visit our website at www.simonspeakers.com.

Series designed by Karin Paprocki

Jacket designed by Nina Simoneaux

The text of this book was set in Belucian Book.

Manufactured in the United States of America 0418 FFG

2 4 6 8 10 9 7 5 3 1

Library of Congress Control Number 2017943952

ISBN 978-1-4814-8712-2 (hc)

ISBN 978-1-4814-8711-5 (pbk)

ISBN 978-1-4814-8713-9 (eBook)

To Ana Fremaint—

so happy you are part of our family

And to Father Robert Hofstetter

Cast of Characters

Shelly

Echo

Kiki

Pearl

Rocky

Contents

A Perfect Solution

WHY ME?" ECHO SAID TO her mother one morning before school. "Why can't Crystal give up her room?"

Mrs. Reef shook her head. "Because your bed is bigger than hers. And it's only for a few days."

Echo wanted to cry and slap her pink tail on the floor, but she knew it wouldn't do any good. Aunt Crabella and Uncle Leopold were coming to visit, and they would sleep in Echo's room. That meant that she'd have to squeeze into her sister's tiny bed. And Crystal snored!

Echo was still unhappy about it on the swim to school. "My mom's sister and her husband are coming to visit this afternoon," she told her best friend, Shelly Siren, as they glided past MerPark. "They've been on vacation and are stopping here on their way home."

"That's nice," Shelly said, dodging left to avoid a diving Risso's dolphin.

"It would be if they weren't sleeping in

my room." Echo scowled. "I have to share Crystal's bed for the next couple of nights, and she barely gives me any space."

"Maybe you could sleep on the sponge couch in your living room?" Shelly suggested. They floated into the front entrance hall of their school, Trident Academy.

Over their heads, the huge shell's ceiling was filled with colorful old carvings of merfolk history.

"That won't work," Echo said. "My parents will be in the living room talking with my aunt and uncle until late each night."

Just then a merboy zoomed past them. "Watch out!" Shelly shouted at Rocky Ridge as he bumped into Echo on his way into the school.

"Sorry!" Rocky called. Shelly and Echo shook their heads and followed Rocky into their classroom. All the other third graders were already seated. Mrs. Karp hung a kelp poster about seabirds just as the conch sounded to start the school day.

"Good morning, class," Mrs. Karp said.

"Today we'll start a new unit of study about birds called albatrosses and petrels. Have any of you seen one?"

Echo wasn't sure if she'd ever glimpsed a bird before, let alone one of the ones her teacher mentioned. But her friend Kiki Coral raised her hand. "I saw a diving petrel once," Kiki said. "It caught a fish. Then it used its wings to swim."

"Birds can't do that," Rocky said with a shake of his head.

"Oh, but some can," Mrs. Karp told the class. "In fact, let's use our trip to the library this morning to find examples of other birds that can swim."

Echo sighed as the class lined up. She was still upset about having to give up her room.

"Echo," Shelly whispered as they drifted down the hall toward the library. "I have a great idea! Why don't you spend the next few nights at my apartment? I have a big bed and my grandfather won't mind."

Echo smiled. "I'd love to!" It was the perfect solution. Echo and Shelly had sleepovers all the time. Echo couldn't wait to ask her mother.

Good Argument

BUT WHY NOT?" ECHO ASKED after school. She'd just told her mother about Shelly's perfect plan.

"Because it would be rude!" Mrs. Reef explained. "Your aunt and uncle only see you a few times a year. I'm sure they'd like to spend time with you."

Echo took a deep breath. She just needed to explain to her mother that Shelly's idea helped everyone. Nobody would be crowded and . . .

"I know you are thinking up a good argument, but don't bother," Mrs. Reef said, sprinkling sea salt on a pan of conger eel steaks for dinner. "You will stay and visit with your family. Now, please set the table . . . and use the good dishes."

Echo was disappointed. She muttered the

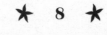

★ 8 ★

entire time she put out plates, forks, knives, and spoons. She was upset as she folded the spectacular seaweed napkins beside each plate. She frowned while she helped her sister make a flatworm and sea lettuce salad.

Finally her mother put her hands on her hips. "Echo, stop sulking around. I'd like you to be in a good mood when your aunt and uncle arrive. Your father will be back from picking them up at the Manta Ray station any merminute now."

Echo started to say that she'd be in a good mood if she didn't have to give up her room, but she didn't. Her mother looked so hopeful that Echo just nodded. "I'll try."

Crystal and Echo were putting vases of eelgrass and sea pink onto the table when

their father swam in the door, followed by Aunt Crabella and Uncle Leopold.

Echo looked up to say hello, but nothing came out. She was too shocked to say a word!

The Hairy Fairy

COME GIVE ME A HUG, ECHO," Aunt Crabella said with her arms outstretched. At least Echo thought it was her aunt, but she was dressed very differently than usual. On top of her head was a huge bag made of seaweed; it was the size of a large blobfish. Her hair wasn't black like it used to be, except for the tips. Instead long braids coated with red clay floated all around her face. Her arms and neck were covered with bracelets and beads. Even her dress was coated with beads. And red clay covered every inch of her aunt's brown skin.

"What happened to you?" Echo said, putting her hands on her hips.

"Echo!" her mother snapped. "That is very rude."

Aunt Crabella chuckled. "Well, I suppose I do look a little different. We've just finished a long ocean trip to the Skeleton Coast and decided to dress a bit like the Himba people we met there. It is quite unique, don't you think?"

Echo nodded. She'd never seen anything like it in her life.

"Did you enjoy your trip?" Crystal asked.

"I think Crabella could have stayed there forever," Uncle Leopold said.

Aunt Crabella nodded, and her clay-covered braids swirled like sea snakes around her face. "You won't believe the amazing stories I have to tell you!"

"Can you tell us one now?" Echo asked. Aunt Crabella always had the best tales.

"Your aunt and uncle need to rest from their long trip," Echo's mother told her.

Aunt Crabella must have noticed Echo's sad face because she said, "After dinner tonight, I'll share the Skeleton Coast legend of the Hairy Fairy."

Echo giggled. "What is a hairy fairy?"

Aunt Crabella scratched at the clay that was cracking on the tip of her nose. "Only the most important fairy to have ever lived."

"Are there really such things as fairies?" Echo asked.

"Of course not," Echo's mother said sharply. "Enough of this silly talk! Now, Echo, show your aunt and uncle to your room."

Echo wondered why her mother didn't want her talking about fairies. But she didn't have time to think about it. As she led her aunt and uncle down the hallway to her room, Uncle Leopold said, "It is very generous of you to let us sleep in your bed."

"Indeed," Aunt Crabella agreed. Her bangle bracelets jingled as she patted Echo's shoulder. "The most powerful fairies love kindness. I'm sure they will reward you with a lovely surprise."

The Legend

AT DINNER UNCLE LEOPOLD took forever to finish his dessert of paddle-weed pudding. Echo thought she would never get to hear her aunt's story. The mersecond her uncle put down his shell spoon, Echo sputtered to her aunt, "Can you tell us the Hairy Fairy legend now?"

Echo's father shook his head. "Echo, you need to learn patience."

"And forget this fairy nonsense!" her mother said firmly.

"Oh, it won't hurt to tell a little story, now, will it?" Aunt Crabella asked. "But Echo, first we must help your parents clean the dishes after they prepared this excellent meal."

Echo held her breath. She thought she might die if she had to wait any longer!

"Fine," Echo's mother said with a sigh. "I'll do the dishes and you can start the story in the living room."

Echo's father winked at her. "I'll help your mother."

"Thanks," Echo said quickly before her parents changed their minds.

Uncle Leopold nodded. "But tomorrow, *we* do the cleaning."

Aunt Crabella settled onto the sponge couch with Uncle Leopold beside her. Echo and Crystal sat on orange lichen throw pillows, gifts their aunt and uncle had brought from the Skeleton Coast. "Okay," Aunt Crabella said, "I was going to tell a story about a shark, right?"

"No!" Echo squealed. "You were going to tell us about the Hairy Fairy."

Aunt Crabella smiled. "Of course. Then let me begin."

She pushed back her clay-covered braids, closed her eyes, and began speaking in a much deeper voice. Echo looked at Crystal in surprise. The low tones of her aunt's voice gave Echo the chills. "There are two kinds of fairies," Aunt Crabella said. "Those who are kind and those who are tricky."

"Which is the Hairy Fairy?" Echo asked.

Aunt Crabella opened her eyes and asked, "What do you think?"

"I bet she's tricky," Crystal answered.

Aunt Crabella nodded and continued, "Her favorite trick is to sneak into merfolk homes and spend the night twisting the hair of young mermaids. The tangles they wake up with are known as fairy locks."

Echo gasped. Almost every morning her black, curly hair was tangled. Had the Hairy Fairy been tricking her?

"What else does she do?" Crystal asked.

"Tell them about the treasure," Uncle Leopold suggested.

"The Hairy Fairy has a treasure?" Echo asked.

Aunt Crabella pointed to one of the bracelets on her arm, a beautiful glittering gold bangle bracelet. "This is from her treasure."

"Sweet seaweed!" Echo whispered.

"Did she give it to you?" Crystal asked.

"Yes, but only after I caught her!" Aunt Crabella replied with a smile. Echo squealed with excitement and begged her aunt to tell them how she caught the Hairy Fairy, but she refused. "Each mermaid must find her own special way to catch a fairy."

Finally Echo's mother came in from the kitchen and clapped her hands. "Enough stories! Echo and Crystal, it's time for you to get ready for bed."

Echo began to argue, but her mother's stern face silenced her. Why didn't her mother like fairies?

That night, however, while Echo changed into her nightgown, she could only think about catching the Hairy Fairy. It would be the most exciting thing ever!

5

Fairy Tern

THAT NIGHT ECHO TRIED very hard to stay awake. She wanted to catch the Hairy Fairy tangling her hair. First she tapped her fingers. Then she swung her tail back and forth under the covers.

She wondered if Aunt Crabella had

snuck up on the Hairy Fairy when she'd caught her. Echo imagined her aunt surprising the fairy by setting a trap. Maybe that's what she could do!

"Stop wiggling!" Crystal snapped from the other side of the bed.

Somehow, even though Echo tried hard not to, she fell asleep anyway. The next thing she knew it was morning and her hair was just as tangled as usual.

At lunch that day, Echo shared her aunt's story of the Hairy Fairy with her friends. "The legend says that if you catch the Hairy Fairy, she will give you some of her treasure. My aunt got a pretty bracelet before the fairy escaped."

"Maybe the Hairy Fairy stole the

treasure from the famous human pirate William Kidd. No one ever found his stolen loot," Kiki said. "Some people say it's hidden off the Skeleton Coast."

"Really?" Echo squealed. She thought people were fascinating, and she was sure that human treasure would be mervelous.

"Why do they call it the Skeleton Coast?" Shelly asked. "That sounds creepy."

Kiki had the answer. "It's named after the shipwrecks and whale bones that washed ashore there."

Echo thought her friends were missing the point. "But what about the Hairy Fairy?" she asked.

Shelly took a bite of her clam casserole before saying, "I'm pretty sure that fairies are make-believe, but it is fun to pretend."

A mergirl named Pearl sniffed as she floated by. "Fairies don't exist! *I've* never seen one."

"Just because you haven't seen one doesn't mean they don't exist," Echo said.

Kiki nodded and her long, dark hair swirled around her. "Echo has a point. We've never seen a human, but we know they are real. Maybe fairies are the same."

"That gives me an idea!" Echo said. "I have to go. See you later." She hopped up from the lunch table and zoomed toward the school library. It was the perfect place to do some research.

With a little help from the librarian, Miss Scylla, Echo was able to find five books about fairies. One said that fairies can make themselves invisible. "Well, that explains why no one sees the Hairy Fairy messing up their hair," Echo said out loud.

Another book scared Echo because it talked about being trapped in fairy rings, circles of Scotch bonnet sea snails. She vowed to watch out for them, and to never step inside one. "Maybe finding a fairy isn't such a good idea after all," she whispered.

A thick blue book said that anyone who ate fairy food in fairyland would be stuck there forever. Echo wondered exactly what fairy food tasted like. What if you ate it by accident?

She felt a bit better when she read in a small red book that some fairies like to leave presents for mermaids to find.

But she slammed the last book shut when she read that anyone who hears fairy music will be forced to dance forever, unless the fairy changes the tune. Echo liked to dance, but she didn't want to do it forever.

After the conch shell rang, Echo swam back to her classroom and tried to concentrate on her lessons. Mrs. Karp asked the class, "What did you all learn about diving birds at the library yesterday?"

"Doesn't the brown pelican dive?" Shelly asked.

"Yes. Very good. Anyone else?" Mrs. Karp glanced around the room.

Wanda waved her hand slowly. "How about the brown booby?"

Rocky snickered at the bird's name, but Mrs. Karp nodded. "That is correct, Wanda. Can you add to our list, Rocky?"

Rocky stopped giggling and got a stricken look on his face. "Um, the white tern?"

"The white tern, also known as the fairy tern, is lovely," Mrs. Karp said. "But it is not a diver."

Rocky glanced at Echo before saying, "I heard that fairies live at the base of Whale Mountain.

Is that true?" Whale Mountain was close to Trident City.

Mrs. Karp shook her head. "If you're speaking about fairy terns, they feed on ocean fish but live on dry land."

Echo stared at Rocky. She had a feeling that he hadn't been talking about birds at all. How did Rocky know about fairies? Had he seen one?

Rainbow Fairy

ROCKY, I HAVE TO TALK TO you," Echo said in the hallway after school.

Rocky shook his head. "Sorry, I have Shell Wars practice right now," he said before zooming away. Shell Wars was a team sport played by whacking shells with long whale-bone sticks.

Echo groaned. She was supposed to go straight home from school to entertain Aunt Crabella and Uncle Leopold until her parents returned from work. She'd have to wait until tomorrow to ask Rocky what he knew about fairies.

Back at her house, Echo quickly did her homework so she could ask her aunt more fairy questions. When she swam into the kitchen, Echo noticed that her uncle was dressed in his normal clothes instead of the colorful garments he'd worn yesterday, but her aunt wasn't around.

"Echo," Uncle Leopold said, "can you

please stir this beadlet anemone soup? We are surprising your parents by making dinner."

"Where's Aunt Crabella?" Echo asked. "I have a question for her."

"She went to Merlin's to pick up some special spices," Uncle Leopold explained. "She'll be home soon."

Echo stirred the soup while Crystal whisked up some white-sea-whip pudding for dessert. It was nearly time to eat when Aunt Crabella finally returned. She wore a brightly colored top, but the clay on her body and hair was gone. "Aunt Crabella," Echo said, "can I ask you something?"

"I'm sorry, but now isn't a good time,"

Aunt Crabella told her. "I want to finish this soup and make deviled frigatebird eggs. Keep stirring the soup while I add this phytoplankton. It will give the broth a rich flavor."

All through dinner, Echo had to listen to her parents discuss boring matters with Aunt Crabella and Uncle Leopold. Echo tried to ask more fairy questions, but her mother gave her a strict look.

Instead of telling stories after dinner, Aunt Crabella wanted to play games. Echo didn't get a chance to ask more about fairies. But she fell asleep thinking about them.

In her dream that night, Echo was a fairy! And not just any fairy, but a fairy princess. She wore a sparkling pink gown to match her tail, and her wings were the most amazing blend of rainbow colors.

A small fairy with bright orange hair fluttered up to her. "Hello, Echo!"

"Hi." Echo stared at the fairy's hair. Not only was it brighter than a clown fish, but it touched the ocean floor and was very, very bushy. In fact, the fairy's hair was almost bigger than she was. It nearly covered her bright blue wings! "Are you the Hairy Fairy?" Echo asked.

Instead of answering her, the fairy just grinned and flew off. Echo tried to catch her, but something had snagged Echo's pink dress. She tugged hard to pull it loose.

The dress jerked away and Echo fell to

the ground with a *plop!* She awoke on the floor of her sister's room with a kelp blanket wrapped around her.

"Hey!" Crystal peered over the side of the bed. "Stop stealing the covers!"

Echo tossed the blanket back on the bed and wondered: Had she really just talked to the Hairy Fairy?

Do You Believe?

ECHO TRIED TO GET BACK TO
sleep but couldn't. She finally
gave up and went into the
kitchen to get a glass of warm kelp juice.
She was surprised to find Aunt Crabella
sitting at the table with a cup of comb-
jelly tea.

"I'm glad you're awake," Echo said. "I wanted to ask you more about fairies."

Aunt Crabella shook her head. "I'm sorry, Echo. Your mother asked me not to tell you any more fairy stories."

"Why not?"

Aunt Crabella took a sip of tea before answering, "Your mother doesn't want me filling your head with something that she thinks is silly."

Echo poured her kelp juice and sat down at the table with a thump. She couldn't understand her mother. What was wrong with believing in fairies? And what right did her mother have to tell Aunt Crabella the kind of stories she could share? Suddenly Echo was very mad at her mother.

Aunt Crabella patted Echo's shoulder. "Now, don't get upset. Your mother has every right to say what happens in her home."

Echo frowned but didn't speak a word.

"Perhaps I shouldn't have told you in the first place," her aunt said with a sigh. "I'm not sure why she gets so upset, but I know your mom doesn't believe in them."

"What about you?" Echo asked. "Do you believe in fairies?"

Aunt Crabella smiled. "Your mother and I are quite different. She is a scientist and I am a travel writer. We look at the world in different ways."

"You didn't answer my question," Echo insisted. "Do you believe in fairies?" She didn't find it silly to think that they might be real, but she wanted to know what her aunt thought.

"Oh, I'm not answering that," Aunt Crabella said. "You have to decide for yourself."

"You sound like my teacher," Echo grumbled.

Her aunt laughed so loudly that Echo

worried she might wake up her parents. To her relief, Aunt Crabella spoke a bit softer when she said, "A famous human writer once wrote, 'Some things have to be believed to be seen.'"

Echo wasn't sure what her aunt meant. After all, Aunt Crabella had seen the Hairy Fairy, or had she made up that story? "So you don't believe in fairies?"

"Oh, I didn't say that." Aunt Crabella shook her head and hugged Echo. "I know how much you like humans, so I'll tell you something else a human writer once said."

Echo was surprised. How did her aunt know so much about people's writing?

"Don't look so shocked. Writing is a very powerful way to share a message, no matter whether you are human or merfolk."

"What did the writer say?" Echo asked.

"'I believe in everything until it's dis-proved. So I believe in fairies, the myths, dragons. It all exists, even if it's in your mind.'"

Echo thought about that for a mer-minute. But before she could ask any more questions, Aunt Crabella got up from the table.

"We'd better get back to bed. And Echo, let's not mention any of this to your mother."

Echo nodded. She didn't want to disobey her mother, but she sure wanted to believe in something as special as fairies. And she really, really wanted to see one!

Fairy Juice

THE NEXT MORNING ECHO pounced on Rocky the mer-minute he floated by her shell on his way to school. "What do you know about fairies?"

"You scared the seaweed out of me!" Rocky yelped, and dropped his schoolbag.

"And what makes you think I know anything about fairies?"

Echo stared at Rocky. "You told Mrs. Karp that fairies live near Whale Mountain."

Rocky shrugged. "Did I say that? I must have read it somewhere."

Echo put her hands on her hips. "What else did you read?"

"That you need fairy juice to catch a fairy." Rocky didn't look at Echo as he grabbed his schoolbag.

"I didn't read anything about that in the library," Echo said. "What book was that in?"

"*Find a Fairy*?" Rocky said.

"I've never seen that book," Echo said.

"Tell me the truth." She wasn't sure if Rocky knew what the truth was exactly. He liked to exaggerate.

"I think my mom might have mentioned it once," Rocky said, looking at the ocean floor.

Echo didn't say anything for a mer-minute. She knew Rocky's mom had died several years ago. For once Echo was pretty sure he was telling the truth. She couldn't resist asking, "Do you know how to make fairy juice?"

Rocky grinned. "I can't tell you right now or we'll be late. Meet me in the front hall after school," he said, and zoomed away.

Echo was so happy she did a backflip. She was going to catch a fairy and prove to her mother that they were real! All she needed was fairy juice!

"Why are you so excited?" Shelly asked, swimming up beside Echo.

"I am going on a fairy chase," Echo said. "Want to come?" She held her breath. After all, Shelly said she didn't believe in fairies.

"That sounds like fun," Shelly said. "Count me in! But for now we'd better get to school."

That morning Echo could hardly pay attention in class. While Mrs. Karp was discussing the laughing gull, Echo was thinking about fairies. Could fairy juice really help her capture one?

At lunch, Kiki shook Echo's shoulder. "Are you all right?"

"I'm fin-tastic," Echo said. "Why do you ask?"

Shelly pointed to Echo's food. "You haven't even touched your hagfish jelly sandwich."

"I was thinking about those human objects that take pictures you can keep," Echo said. "I wish I had one." It would be perfect for when she caught a fairy. After all, it wouldn't be right to keep a fairy trapped for long, but a picture could last forever!

"I think they're called cameras," Kiki told her. "But some artists can draw pictures that look like the real thing, like the artist at Neptune's Castle."

Echo nodded, remembering the merman

who had sketched the mergirls before their very first fancy ball. "That's a mervelous idea," she said.

"What are you going to draw?" Shelly asked.

"Well, I hope you guys will help me capture a fairy after school, and then I'm going to sketch it," Echo exclaimed. "All we need is fairy juice!"

Rocky's Recipe

WASN'T IT NICE OF Rocky to share his mom's recipe for fairy juice?" Echo said later that afternoon. Shelly, Echo, and Kiki were in Echo's kitchen, mixing the ingredients for Rocky's recipe. Crystal had agreed to entertain

Aunt Crabella and Uncle Leopold in the living room so Echo and her friends could make the juice and then go on a fairy chase.

Kiki scrunched up her nose. "It's hard to believe fairies like this stuff. It smells terrible!"

"You don't think he's teasing us, do you? What if he made this whole thing up?" Shelly asked.

Echo shook her head, but then she wondered. Rocky had given her the recipe, but he'd said he was too busy to make the juice or hunt for fairies with them. "No," she decided finally. "He wants to help."

Shelly stirred the thick, greenish-purple concoction of sea-hare ink and algae. "Maybe fairies don't have noses."

"They do," Echo said.

"How do you know?" Kiki asked.

"I dreamed about one," Echo said. "But it seemed so real that I'm actually not sure if it was a dream or if the Hairy Fairy was really there. She definitely had a nose and very long orange hair."

Shelly stopped stirring to look at Echo. "Do you truly believe in fairies?" she asked.

Echo remembered Aunt Crabella's words and said, "I believe in everything until it's proven wrong. So I believe in fairies, the myths, and dragons."

Shelly looked at Kiki, who was holding her nose. "Kiki, do you believe in fairies?"

Kiki shrugged. "What does it hurt?" Because she was still holding her nose, it sounded like, "Whaa dud ick hurrrr?"

Shelly and Echo laughed. "Do you think this fairy juice is ready?" Shelly asked.

The three mergirls stared into the bowl.

"Ick!" Kiki gasped at the nasty smell.

"It's done," Echo said firmly. "Now, let's go catch a fairy!"

Something Stinky

ECHO CARRIED THE STINKY bowl as far from her body as she could, but by the time the mergirls got to Whale Mountain, she felt like she was going to be sick from the horrible smell. The mountain was just a short swim outside Trident City, but it seemed much farther.

"Let me hold that for a bit," Shelly said. Echo gratefully gave the fairy juice to her best friend.

Kiki covered her nose and tried to stay as far from the nasty mess as possible. "I'm sorry, but that smell makes me want to throw up."

"It's okay," Shelly said with a giggle. "It's not much worse than my grandpa's dirty work shirts."

"So, where should we look?" Echo asked. "Rocky didn't say exactly where the fairies might be."

Kiki took her hand off her nose long

enough to say, "Let's swim around a little bit."

The mergirls glided to the left side of the sperm-whale-shaped mountain. They had just passed a big clump of brown horn-wrack when Shelly pointed to a small fin-like rock above them. "Look!"

Echo couldn't believe her eyes. It was the most beautiful thing she'd ever seen. A magical fairy forest of purple sea urchins and sea lilies framed dozens of tiny fairies with blue, green, yellow, and purple wings. They were even prettier than the library books' pictures.

The mergirls were perfectly still as the fairies moved around the fairy forest, their miniature wings bobbing gently in the water. Their bodies were humanlike, only much more delicate. Echo felt like she was dreaming. She couldn't believe she was seeing fairies!

"They're so lovely," Kiki said softly. "Almost too lovely to be real."

"Look," Echo whispered. "There's a tiny fairy in that little house." The house was barely bigger than her fist, and it was made entirely of seashells and moss. Through the arched door and open windows, Echo could see pink wings fluttering about.

"Should we get nearer so we can draw pictures?" Shelly asked.

Echo definitely wanted to get closer. She longed to catch a fairy and keep it for the

rest of her life. And if she did, she might even get a treasure!

But something stopped her. The fairies were so dainty that Echo didn't want to scare them. She wanted to protect them. She decided that just seeing them was treasure enough.

"No," Echo said in the quietest voice she could muster. "Let's draw them from here." Her friends didn't argue. Echo thought they must have felt the same way.

Shelly put the stinky bowl of fairy juice behind a rock. The three mergirls peeked around a barrel sponge to sketch the fairies, using octopus ink on kelp pads. Echo's hands were shaking so much from excitement that it was hard to draw straight lines, but she did her best. First she studied the pink fairy and then she tried to draw it exactly as she saw it.

But when Echo drew the fairy's wings, she noticed that something was wrong . . . terribly wrong!

A Trick!

ECHO SOARED THROUGH THE water toward the fairies. She wasn't afraid of scaring them anymore. Now she was mad! And she was going to catch someone—only that some-one wasn't a fairy!

She reached around a rock and yanked a brown tail.

"Ouch!" screamed Rocky. "Let go!"

Kiki and Shelly swam up beside Echo. Rocky came out from behind the rock with an embarrassed look on his face.

"What's going on?" Shelly asked.

Echo pointed to the wispy, thin strands of seaweed that were attached to the fairies. "Rocky used these to move the fairy dolls around so we would think they were real." She felt like crying. How could Rocky trick them like that?

"That was a rotten thing to do," Shelly told him.

"I wasn't trying to be

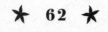

★ 62 ★

mean," Rocky said. "I heard Echo telling a fairy story in the lunchroom yesterday."

"So you thought you would make fun of me? Were you going to tease me about it later?" Echo could barely keep tears from spilling down her cheeks.

"No, I wasn't going to tease you," Rocky said.

"You made us whip up that stinky fairy juice for nothing!" Shelly snapped.

"It was disgusting!" Kiki agreed. "I almost threw up."

Rocky's face turned red. "Oops. I just needed to keep you busy for a few mer-minutes so I could put the fairies in place. I didn't think about how the juice would smell."

"Come on, Echo," Kiki said. "Let's get out of here."

"I'm sorry if I hurt your feelings!" Rocky told them before they could leave. "It's just that your fairy story reminded me of my mom. We used to play with these when I was little. My mom loved fairies; she collected these dolls. I thought Echo might like them."

It wasn't like Rocky to apologize. Was he telling the truth?

Echo opened her mouth to yell at Rocky, but she saw something that changed her mind. A small tear pooled in the corner of one of Rocky's eyes. She knew that Rocky really missed his mom. Maybe he just wanted a friend who would play fairies with him.

Echo took a deep breath and smiled at Rocky. "That's okay," she told him. Kiki and Shelly gave her shocked looks. "I don't like the way you tricked us, but maybe we could play with the fairies sometime?"

Rocky grinned. "That sounds like a fairy good plan!" he said, and the mergirls laughed.

Real Fun

THE NEXT AFTERNOON A tiny shell opened right in front of Echo's eyes. Then a purple fairy showed Echo a tiny treasure chest filled with sparkling pebbles.

"Wow! They're beautiful," Echo said.

Echo and Rocky were at Rocky's, playing

with his mother's fairy dolls. Suddenly a green fairy landed beside the shell. Echo worried that the new fairy would take away the treasure, but Rocky surprised her.

"Today is a special day in fairyland," he said, pretending to be the green fairy. "All visitors get to take two fairies home to spend the night."

"Really?" Echo said. She couldn't believe Rocky would let her borrow some of his mother's beautiful fairies. They were all so pretty; how could she pick? She finally decided on one small pink and one purple fairy.

After saying good-bye to Rocky, Echo swam home, carrying the fairies carefully in her arms. She was only sorry that

Aunt Crabella and Uncle Leopold had left that morning. They would have loved to see the fairies.

Unfortunately, her mother met her at the door. "There you are! Dinner's almost ready." She peered down at Echo's arms. "What's that?" she asked.

"Fairies," Echo said, looking at the little dolls. She wished she had thought of hiding them. Would her mother make her take them back to Rocky? Would she throw them away? Echo's heart pounded.

But instead her mother burst into tears. Echo felt terrible. "What's wrong?" she asked. "Is it the fairies? I'll take them back to Rocky's house. He let me borrow them."

Her mother wiped the tears from her

eyes. "No," she said. "You don't have to take them back."

"I know you don't like fairies," Echo said.

"It's not that," her mother said. "I used to play with those exact same fairies many, many years ago with Rocky's mother."

"You?" Echo said. "But I thought you didn't believe in fairies. You're a scientist!"

Mrs. Reef shrugged. "Well, scientists can have fun too. It's just that I was good friends with Rocky's mom when I was a young fry, and I miss her. It was painful for me to think about fairies without her."

"I'm sorry," Echo said. She hadn't meant to upset her mother.

Mrs. Reef shook her head. "It was sad, but not anymore. Seeing my favorite fairies reminds me of all the fun we used to have with them. Rocky's mom would have wanted these fairies to be played with."

"So you're not mad at me for believing in fairies?" Echo asked.

"Of course not," Mrs. Reef said. "But there is one thing I'd like you to do."

"What's that?"

Mrs. Reef smiled. "Play fairies with me this afternoon!"

Echo laughed. She wasn't sure whether fairies were real, but playing with Rocky and then with her mother was a different kind of real. Real fun!

Class
Reports

SHELLY SIREN

My True or False About the Common Eider

1. This duck dives to catch mollusks and crabs.

2. The female has a green neck.

3. Eiderdown is made from its feathers. It makes soft pillows!

Answers: 1. True 2. False (male has a green neck) 3. True

Echo Reef

My True or False about the *Fairy Prion*

1. This bird eats other birds.

2. It is a diving bird.

3. It has an M shape on its back and wings.

Answers: 1. False (it eats planktonic animals) 2. False 3. True

ROCKY

My True or False About the Common Loon

1. This bird can dive deeper than the length of two blue whales.

2. It is supposed to have a very creepy cry.

3. This bird is purple.

Answers: 1. True (it can dive to 250 feet) 2. True 3. False (it is black and white or brownish-black and gray)

PEARL SWAMP

My True or False About the Guanay
Cormorant

1. It looks a little like a penguin and has a
red patch around each eye.

2. It can swim with its legs.

3. Humans used to collect its poop!

Answers: 1. True 2. True 3. True
(Isn't that disgusting? Humans used the
Guanay cormorant's poop,
or guano, to help grow
their food. Ick!!)

KIKI CORAL

My True or False about the Osprey

1. This bird plunges into the water feet first.

2. It can catch fish that weigh almost as much as it does.

3. Human chemicals do not hurt it.

Answers: 1. True 2. True 3. False (There was once a thing called DDT that really hurt its numbers.)

The Mermaid Song

REFRAIN:

Let the water roar

Deep down we're swimming along

Twirling, swirling, singing the mermaid song.

VERSE 1:

Shelly flips her tail

Racing, diving, chasing a whale

Twirling, swirling, singing the mermaid song.

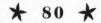

VERSE 2:

Pearl likes to shine

Oh my Neptune, she looks so fine

Twirling, swirling, singing the mermaid song.

VERSE 3:

Shining Echo flips her tail

Backward and forward without fail

Twirling, swirling, singing the mermaid song.

VERSE 4:

 Amazing Kiki

Far from home and floating so free

Twirling, swirling, singing the mermaid song.

Author's Note

BECAUSE I LIKE TO WRITE about mermaids, people often ask me if I believe in them. I must admit that I love to believe they are real! After all, there is much of the ocean that has never been explored. Who knows what creatures are waiting to be discovered?

The two quotes that Aunt Crabella mentioned in the story are real ones. A children's author named Madeleine

L'Engle said, "Some things have to be believed to be seen," which is a twist on what people usually say—you have to see it to believe it. The other quote is by John Lennon, who was a member of a famous band called the Beatles. He said, "I believe in everything until it's disproved. So I believe in fairies, the myths, dragons. It all exists, even if it's in your mind."

So I believe in mermaids and fairies. How about you?

Your mermaid friend,
Debbie

Glossary

ALBATROSS: The black-browed albatross is also called the black-browed molly-mawk. Groups of them can often be seen following ships.

ALGAE: A type of algae named *Emiliania huxleyi* smells like rotten eggs!

BARREL SPONGE: The barrel sponge grows so big that a person could actually fit inside it!

BEADLET ANEMONE: If you see a blob of what looks like red or green jelly on a rocky shoreline, it might just be a beadlet anemone, which has stinging cells at the top of its body. Luckily, the sting isn't harmful to humans.

BLOBFISH: This fish, commonly found off the coast of Australia, truly looks like a blob!

BROWN BOOBY: This bird is a spectacular diver, dropping from heights of up to a hundred feet, which is almost as high as three telephone poles stacked on top of one another.

CLAM: There are more than fourteen thousand types of clams and their relatives. They have a two-piece shell, held together by a hinge.

CLOWN FISH: Clown fish, or anemonefish, are known for being bright orange, but they can also be yellow, red, or black. They have a symbiotic relationship with anemones.

CONGER EEL: This snakelike fish likes to hide in holes. Many divers see them sticking their heads out of wrecked ships.

COMB JELLY: The predatory comb jelly has long arms, or tentacles, that are sticky to help it catch food.

DWARF SPERM WHALE: The dwarf sperm whale is the smallest whale. It is smaller than some dolphins.

EELGRASS: This sea grass has long, ribbon-like leaves and grows in both cold waters and tropical seas.

FAIRY TERN: This bird is completely white, except for its black eyes and bill. It is also called the white tern.

FRIGATEBIRD: The great frigatebird has extremely long wings and can soar for hours above the ocean with just a flick of its wings. Males have bright red throat pouches, which they use to attract female birds.

HAGFISH: This long fish can tie itself in knots! It spends most of the time in the mud and regularly squeezes slime out of its body.

HORNWRACK: This animal is often mistaken for brown seaweed and looks like clumps of brown lettuce.

KELP: Giant kelp grows amazingly fast. It can grow longer than two school buses in just one year!

LAUGHING GULL: This black-capped bird often follows fishing boats and can be found on beaches, looking for food.

FLATWORM: Flatworms have very thin bodies. You can even see through some of them.

LICHEN: Lichen can grow in some of the most hostile environments in the world, including the heat of the Skeleton Coast.

MANTA RAY: This is the biggest ray in the world. But don't worry, it only eats plankton and small fish.

MOSS: Seaside moss grows along the shore and is sometimes covered by high tides.

OCTOPUS: The smart giant octopus squirts a cloud of purple ink when it is frightened.

PADDLE WEED: This type of seaweed is an important food for the dugong, a marine mammal that is about the size of a manatee.

PETREL: This seabird only goes on land to have babies. It can remain in the air for days at a time.

PHYTOPLANKTON: Phytoplankton are tiny green floating plants that make much of the world's oxygen and are food for many ocean creatures.

PURPLE SEA URCHIN: The sea urchin's favorite food is giant kelp, and it has been responsible for killing off large parts of the kelp forest near the North American coast.

RISSO'S DOLPHIN: This large blackish-blue dolphin has a square head and is also called a gray grampus.

SCOTCH BONNET: This sea snail's pretty shell looks like a traditional Scottish bonnet or cap.

SEA LETTUCE: This green seaweed grows on seashores and is a popular food for humans in some parts of the world.

SEA LILY: Sea lilies cannot swim but can drag themselves along the seabed with their arms.

SEA PINK: This bright pink flower grows along seashores.

SEA SNAKE: The olive sea snake can be brown or olive-brown and lives in the Indian Ocean and western Pacific. It is nosy and often approaches divers, but it will bite if provoked!

SHARK: The scalloped hammerhead shark has an unusual T-shaped, or hammer-shaped, head.

SPECTACULAR SEAWEED: This colorful seaweed grows in deep water. Young plants are a purple-bluish color.

SPERM WHALE: The sperm whale is the largest of the toothed whales and has a huge, squared head.

SPONGE: The Mediterranean bath sponge is soft and was once used as a bath sponge by humans.

WHITE SEA WHIP: Sea whips look like long, thin fingers growing out of the seabed.

Turn the page for a peek at

Book 1 of the Mermaid Tales:

Trouble at Trident Academy

I CAN'T BELIEVE IT!" ECHO SAID. "IT'S finally happening."

Shelly took a small sip of her seaweed juice before pushing a lock of red hair from her face. Usually she didn't care if her hair stuck straight up, but today was special. "We're so lucky to get an invitation to Trident Academy. I didn't think it would happen to me."

Echo and Shelly both lived in Trident City, not far from the famous Trident Academy. They had been friends since they'd played together in the small-fry area of MerPark. The eight-year-old mermaids were celebrating their first day of school with breakfast at the Big Rock Café, a favorite hangout. The place was packed with students proudly wearing their Trident Academy sashes. The two mergirls didn't see a third mergirl swimming up behind them. Her name was Pearl. Echo and Shelly usually tried to avoid the bossy mergirl from their neighborhood.

"Oh my Neptune!" Pearl snapped when

she saw Shelly. "I can't believe *you*, of all merpeople, got into Trident." Usually only very wealthy or extremely smart students were accepted. Pearl was rich. Echo was a quick learner. Shelly was neither, but she knew more about ocean animals than both of them put together.

Echo came to her friend's defense. "Of course Shelly got into Trident. She is very talented."

"At *what*?" Pearl asked. "Digging for crabs?"

Shelly glanced at her dirty fingernails and immediately hid them under her blue tail fin. "At least I know *how* to hunt crabs. I bet you'd starve to death if you had to do something for yourself."

Pearl flipped her blond hair, stuck her pointy nose up in the water, and said, "I know how to do plenty of things."

"Name one," Shelly said.

"How to be on time for school, for starters," she said. Pearl spun around and flicked her gold tail, knocking seaweed juice all over Shelly's new Trident sash!

Splash!

Pearl giggled and swam off toward school.

"Oh no!" Shelly squealed, dabbing green juice off the gold-and-blue sash. "She did that on purpose!"

Echo glared after Pearl before helping her friend wipe the sash. "It's fine now. You can hardly see it," Echo said. That wasn't *exactly* true—there was definitely a green blob on Shelly's sash.

"We'd better get going," Echo said, adjusting the glittering plankton bow in her dark curly hair. "We don't want to be late on our first day."

Shelly groaned. She wasn't quite so excited now. "If Trident Academy is filled with merpeople like Pearl, then I don't think I'm going to like it."

"There's only one way to find out," Echo said, taking a deep breath. "Let's go."